DUDLEY SCHOOLS
LIBRARY SERVICE

KU-424-882

Schools Library and Information Services

S00000719143

For Lily and Elena -S.C.

For Derek -L.C.

DRAGON'S DINNER
by Susannah Corbett
and Lynne Chapman

First published in 2009 by
Hodder Children's Books

Text copyright © Susannah Corbett 2009
Illustrations copyright © Lynne Chapman 2009

Hodder Children's Books
338 Euston Road, London NW1 3BH

Hodder Children's Books Australia
Level 17/207 Kent Street, Sydney NSW 2000

The right of Susannah Corbett to be identified
as the author and Lynne Chapman as the illustrator
of this Work has been asserted by them in accordance
with the Copyright, Designs and Patents Act 1988.

All rights reserved

A catalogue record of this book is
available from the British Library.

ISBN: 978 0 340 94422 6
10 9 8 7 6 5 4 3 2 1

Printed in China
Colour Reproduction by Dot Gradations Ltd, UK
Hodder Children's Books is a division of Hachette Children's Books.
An Hachette UK Company.
www.hachette.co.uk

DUDLEY PUBLIC LIBRARIES

L

719143   SOH

JYCOR

www.lynnechapman.co.uk

SUSANNAH CORBETT
DRAGON'S DINNER

Illustrated by
LYNNE CHAPMAN

h
Hodder Children's Books

A division of Hachette Children's Books

z z z z z z z z z z z

Deep in the woods in a cave inky black,
A dragon was snoring away on his back.

ZZZZZZZZZ

His yellow eyes opened
the tiniest crack,
And he said to himself,
'I fancy
    a snack.'

Just round the corner
not far from his lair,
The dragon bumped into
a grizzly bear.

'Mr Bear,'
said the dragon,
'now I've got a hunch,
That soon you and I will
be off to do lunch.'

Away ran the
bear through
the perilous wood.
But the dragon
was chasing,

which couldn't
be good.

They hurtled past bushes
and up over rocks,

But as they
jumped down they
bumped into a fox.

They ran from the dragon,
he'd show them no pity,

They ran,
and they ran
and bumped
into a kitty.

'Hello Mr Kitty, you may have nine lives, But you'll need to have TEN if you want to survive.'

They ran from the fiend,
whose breath was
quite foul,

And up to a tree,
where they woke up an owl.

'I think you shall make
such a grand appetiser,
For owls may be wise but
dragons are wiser.'

At the edge of the wood
lived a little grey mouse.
He was busy at work,
painting his house.

From out of the wood
came a terrible crash,
And a huge ball of fire
rose up in a flash.

'Well,' said the mouse,
as he cleared things away,
'That's something you really
don't see every day.'

Out from the wood ran
the fox and the bear,
As the mouse cleaned his
tools with some
patience and care.

Out from the wood ran
the cat and the owl,
As the mouse wiped the
paint off his paws
with a towel.

Out came the dragon,
who was now in a mood,
And getting quite
tired from chasing
his food.

'Aha, little mouse,
when it comes to the crunch,
Barbecue mouse is my
favourite for lunch.'

'Ha ha!' laughed the mouse,
'you're really a dummy.
There's no way that I'm ending
up in your tummy.'

He ran
at the dragon -
grabbed onto
a scale,

And started
to climb up the leathery tail.

The dragon
SNEEZED out
a great jet
of fire,
But the
mouse kept
on climbing
higher
and
higher.

The mouse reached the top
and showing no fear,
Gave one more big leap
and plopped into his ear.

'Well, Mr Dragon you have
got a cheek.
I'll stay in your ear and I'll
SQUEAK and I'll
SQUEAK.'

The squeak was
just small,
no more than
a niggle,
But the dragon
began to
twitch and to wriggle.

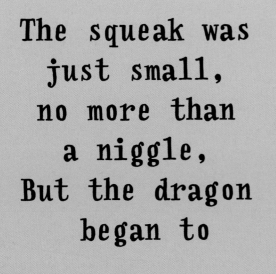

He flew in a circle
and tried a
FLIP FLOP,
But the squeak
in his ear
it just wouldn't stop.

Away ran the dragon
clutching his head.
'Tomorrow,'
he thought,
'I'll just stay in bed.'

'But he's just a mouse,'
sneered the cat. 'He's so weak.'
They looked at the mouse,
and the mouse whispered,

'SQUEAK!'

Away ran the cat and
away ran the bear,
As the mouse settled down
in his favourite chair.

Away flew the owl
and away ran the fox,
As the mouse got
his paper, his ink
and his box.

Away ran the four with
a pitiful wail.
And the mouse dipped his pen,
and wrote us this tale.